MW01242106

Violence Against Women

Public Health and Human Rights

A YOUNG WOMAN'S GUIDE
TO CONTEMPORARY ISSUES™

Violence Against Women

PUBLIC HEALTH AND HUMAN RIGHTS

LINDA BICKERSTAFF

ROSEN
PUBLISHING®

New York

To Gail, a great friend and a survivor of domestic violence

Published in 2010 by The Rosen Publishing Group, Inc.
29 East 21st Street, New York, NY 10010

First Edition

Library of Congress Cataloging-in-Publication Data

Bickerstaff, Linda.
Violence against women: public health and human rights / Linda Bickerstaff. — 1st ed.
     p. cm. (A young woman's guide to contemporary issues)
Includes bibliographical references and index.
ISBN 978-1-4358-3539-9 (library binding)
1. Women—Violence against. I. Title.
HV6250.4.W65B517 2010
362.88082—dc22

2009012062

Manufactured in Malaysia

CPSIA Compliance Information: Batch #TW10YA: For Further Information contact Rosen Publishing, New York, New York at 1-800-237-9932

Contents

PSYCHOLOGICAL   human rights   ABUSIVE BEHAVIORS

DOMESTIC   POWER   dysfunctional

women   VIOLENCE   STEREOTYPES   FEMALE

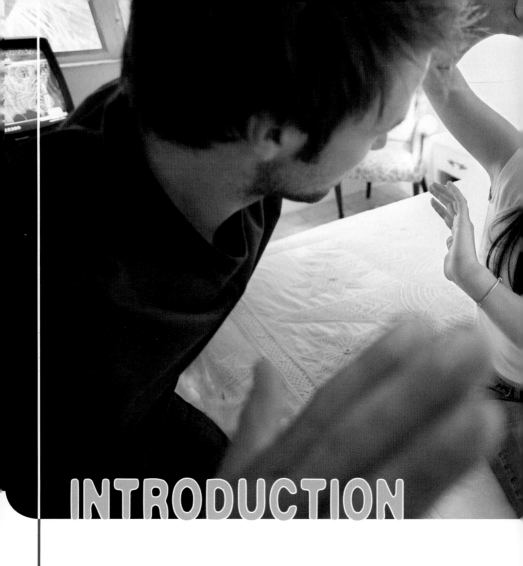

INTRODUCTION

Violence against women is a crime punishable by law and a major public health issue. It is also a violation of the human rights of many women and girls in the United States and throughout the world. But what constitutes violence against women? A widely used definition of violence against women was given in resolution 48/104, passed by the United Nations General Assembly in 1993. The Declaration of the Elimination of Violence Against Women says that

IT MAY BE JUST A SLAP. IT COULD BE RAPE OR EVEN MURDER. ONE IN FOUR AMERICAN WOMEN WILL BE THE VICTIM OF SOME FORM OF VIOLENCE WITHIN HER LIFETIME.

violence against women is any act or even the threat of an act against a girl or woman that results in physical, sexual, or emotional harm. The definition applies whether the act occurs in the privacy of a home or in a school, church, office, or other public place. This definition is the one that is used in this book's discussion of violence against girls and women in the United States.

Violence against women probably dates back to prehistoric times. It has been documented and condoned in ancient writings and in religious books such as the Bible and the Qur'an (Koran), the holy book of the Islamic religion. It has been justified by customs and by laws. It is rooted in the belief that women are subordinate to, or of less value, than men.

When colonists came to America, the laws that they developed reflected the laws they had known before they immigrated. Based on these laws, colonial American women had legal status similar to that of slaves, servants, and children, and only a few more freedoms. Women and girls were accused of witchcraft and other practices for which there was no proof. They were condemned to death by men who made and enforced the laws. Wife beating, called chastisement, was considered a husband's right and was legal in the United States until the early 1870s. Until the 1970s, just forty years ago, the law turned a blind eye to most violence against women. Fortunately, men and women who felt that women were being discriminated against in the United States banded together to start the feminist movement. This movement led the fight to stop violence against women that continues today.

Every girl and woman in the world is at risk of being a victim of violence. Thalif Deen, the United Nations bureau chief for the Inter Press Service (IPS), in "Rights: U.N. Takes Lead on Ending Gender Violence," reports that United Nations secretary-general Ban Ki-moon claims that one out of every three females in the world will be beaten, will be forced into having sex, or will be otherwise abused in her lifetime. Based on projected census data for 2010, Secretary-General Ban Ki-moon's estimates mean that 52.7 million girls and women in the United States and 1.2 billion worldwide may eventually be victims of violence if something is not done to stop it.

With rare exceptions, the perpetrators of violence against girls and women are men. Jackson Katz, in his book *The Macho Paradox*, says that 90 percent of acts of violence against women occur at the hands of men. Ninety-nine percent of rapists are men. Who are these men? They are fathers, brothers, uncles, teachers, the guys next door, or any man.

Girls and women in the United States may be subjected to violence at home, while out with friends, at work, or when they least expect it. Women in the U.S. military are as likely to be harmed by their comrades as by the enemy. By looking at the similarities and the differences among many types of violence against women, people can gain a better understanding of what the challenges are for stopping it. Although efforts to fight violence against girls and women are being made at all levels of government, programs initiated by and for teens, which will be covered later in this book, may ultimately prove to have the greatest effect on achieving this goal.

CHAPTER 1

DOMESTIC VIOLENCE

Domestic violence is sometimes referred to as intimate partner violence. It is defined by the U.S. Justice Department's Office on Violence Against Women as a pattern of abusive behavior, in any relationship, that is used by one partner to gain power and control over the other partner. The word "intimate" is often used to imply a sexual relationship between two people. In this case, the word has a broader meaning. It means a relationship between familiar people, such as family members, husbands, boyfriends, children, or even caregivers.

Domestic violence is the most common type of violence directed toward girls and women. The actual incidence of domestic violence in the United States is hard to determine because it is underreported. The Family Violence Prevention Fund (a U.S. organization that works to end violence against women and children around the world) reports that as many as three million girls and women are subjected to domestic violence each year in the United States. As with

RELATIONAL AGGRESSION: A COVERT TYPE OF EMOTIONAL VIOLENCE

The word "violence" usually calls to mind some type of physical act in which a person is injured. Acts that lead to emotional injuries can also be devastating. Their effects may be as long lasting as those caused by physical violence. A particularly hurtful type of emotional violence is relational aggression (RA). Researchers N. R. Crick and J. K. Grotpeter defined RA as "behavior intended to harm someone by damaging or manipulating his or her relationship with others." It is considered to be a type of bullying. RA happens more often among girls and is being seen at younger and younger ages. Examples of relational aggression include the following:

- Spreading rumors about another person
- Making fun of another person
- Calling another person by a nasty name
- Excluding another person from a group or an activity
- Revealing secrets that have been entrusted to you by another person
- Making mean jokes about another person

Consequences of RA may include depression, anxiety, academic and social problems, misuse of drugs and alcohol, isolation, self-esteem issues, dropping out of school, and even suicide. A girl who is a victim of RA is more likely to become a victim of other kinds of violence as a teen and later as an adult.

Two programs that are dedicated to raising public awareness about RA are the Ophelia Project and the Empower Program. The goal of these programs is to educate parents, schools, and communities about peer aggression and its potential serious consequences.

nearly all types of violence against women and girls, men are usually the perpetrators.

RECOGNIZING DOMESTIC VIOLENCE

More often than not, domestic violence starts quietly. Jealousy is frequently the main reason for domestic violence.

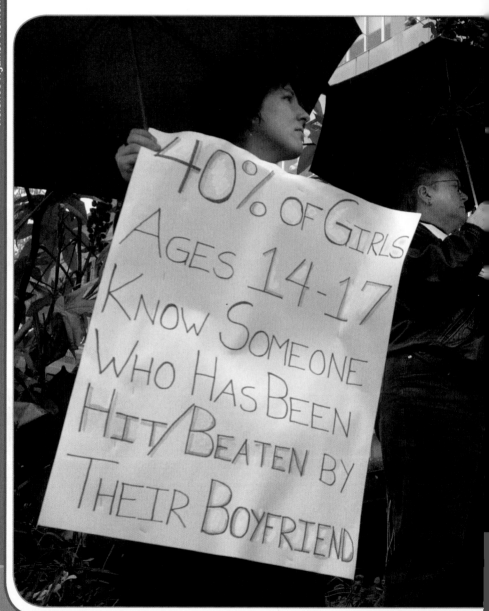

It can start with something as simple as a boyfriend being excessively jealous of his girlfriend's friends. In other cases, it can start with a husband criticizing a meal that his wife has spent all day preparing. The violence usually worsens with each episode. It will involve a combination of several abusive behaviors. These are explained in detail in an article on domestic violence published by the Office on Violence Against Women and include physical abuse, sexual abuse, emotional abuse, economic abuse, and psychological abuse.

Physical abuse, the use of physical force against someone in a manner that harms or endangers that person, is often a component of domestic violence. Hitting, shoving, biting, slapping, beating, cutting, shooting, or being forced to drink alcohol or take drugs are some examples of physical abuse. Sometimes

BRAVING THE RAIN, DEMONSTRATORS OUTSIDE THE COUNTY COURTHOUSE IN MADISON, WISCONSIN, PROTEST FEDERAL FUNDING CUTS FOR PROGRAMS TO PROTECT VICTIMS OF DOMESTIC VIOLENCE.

physical abuse is so extreme that a girl or woman will require emergency medical attention for her injuries or she may die from them. Experts at the Family Violence Prevention Fund say that on average, three girls or women are murdered by their boyfriends or husbands each day in the United States.

Sexual abuse is frequently a factor in domestic violence. It can range from verbal abuse of a sexual nature to unwanted touching to rape.

Emotional abuse occurs in all domestic violence situations. A victim of domestic violence who is told each day how worthless she is may lose her sense of self-respect. Her partner often convinces her that the entire situation is her fault. She may be so ashamed that she will cut herself off from friends and family members. Emotional damage can last a lifetime—long after physical injuries are healed.

Economic, or financial, abuse occurs when the abusive partner maintains complete control over the couple's finances. The woman is given a small amount of money for household expenses and must account for every penny of it. Economic abuse can also involve stealing if the abuser actually removes money from joint bank accounts or sells mutually owned property without the consent of the victim of the abuse. This happens all too often in domestic violence involving older women who cannot care for themselves. Another manifestation of economic abuse occurs if women and girls are kept from furthering their educations or getting jobs that would allow them to be

ABUSIVE RELATIONSHIPS CAN BE PARTICULARLY DAMAGING TO
CHILDREN. MORE THAN HALF OF MEN WHO ABUSE THEIR FEMALE
PARTNERS ALSO ABUSE THEIR CHILDREN.

financially independent. Economic abuse is a major factor for women who want to escape abusive relationships. They often have no money or any way to earn money to support themselves outside of the relationship.

Psychological abuse, like emotional abuse, occurs in almost every domestic violence situation. The most frequent

type of psychological abuse is intimidation. The abuser uses threats of physical violence against his partner, his children, or other family members to maintain control. He may also destroy property that his partner values. An especially cruel type of psychological abuse is the injuring or killing of a pet that is much loved by the victim. An abuser may also

inflict psychological abuse by locking his victim in the house and not letting her out unless he is present.

WHAT'S IT ALL ABOUT?

Domestic violence often occurs in dysfunctional relationships in which partners cannot or will not communicate. It may also occur if men have not learned appropriate ways to handle stress and anger. The so-called cycle of abuse, often discussed as a characteristic of domestic

TO CALL ATTENTION TO THE PLIGHT OF WOMEN ENMESHED IN ABUSIVE RELATIONSHIPS, THE CLOTHESLINE PROJECT DISPLAYS SHIRTS DESIGNED BY WOMEN SURVIVORS OF VIOLENCE.

violence, is a manifestation of this inappropriate response to stress and anger. An article from the Mayo Clinic describes how this cycle of abuse often works. It begins with the abuser getting angry and striking out at the victim with either words or actions or both. After this explosion of anger, the abuser appears to be ashamed, begs for forgiveness, and promises it will never happen again. He may even claim that he does not remember getting angry and acting violently. A peaceful period, often called a honeymoon period, follows. The victim of the violence begins to hope that all is well in the relationship. The abuser then gets angry again and the entire cycle is repeated. A woman may view her partner's "amnesia" about the anger and violence as a manifestation of illness in her abuser. Because she believes that her abusive partner is ill, she may choose to stay in the relationship.

According to an article from the London Abused Women's Center (LAWC) in Ontario, Canada, many abused women think that the notion of the cycle of abuse is nonsense. Abuse is always present at some level or another. For instance, during the so-called honeymoon period, the good times are overshadowed by the fear of impending violence and the stress of not knowing when it will erupt again. To these victims, the stress of not knowing when they will be abused is worse than the abuse itself.

Many abused women also argue that intimate partner violence is systematic and intentional and not just something that happens spontaneously. For example, if a man

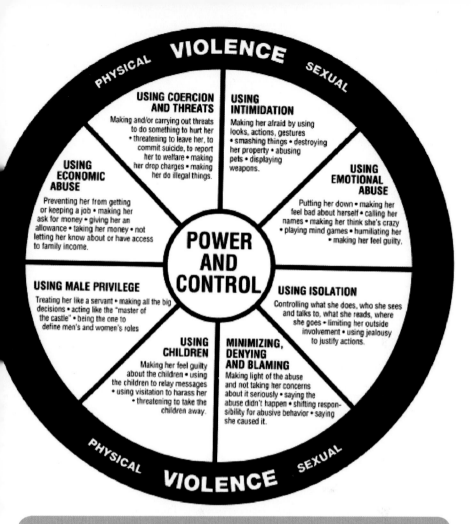

USING COERCION
AND THREATS
Making and/or carrying out threats
to do something to hurt her
• threatening to leave her, to
commit suicide, to report
her to welfare • making
her drop charges • making
her do illegal things.

USING
INTIMIDATION
Making her afraid by using
looks, actions, gestures
• smashing things • destroying
her property • abusing
pets • displaying
weapons.

USING
ECONOMIC
ABUSE
Preventing her from getting
or keeping a job • making her
ask for money • giving her an
allowance • taking her money • not
letting her know about or have access
to family income.

USING
EMOTIONAL
ABUSE
Putting her down • making her
feel bad about herself • calling her
names • making her think she's crazy
• playing mind games • humiliating her
• making her feel guilty.

POWER
AND
CONTROL

USING MALE PRIVILEGE
Treating her like a servant • making all the big
decisions • acting like the "master of
the castle" • being the one to
define men's and women's roles

USING ISOLATION
Controlling what she does, who she sees
and talks to, what she reads, where
she goes • limiting her outside
involvement • using jealousy
to justify actions.

USING
CHILDREN
Making her feel guilty
about the children • using
the children to relay messages
• using visitation to harass her
• threatening to take the
children away.

MINIMIZING,
DENYING
AND BLAMING
Making light of the abuse
and not taking her concerns
about it seriously • saying the
abuse didn't happen • shifting responsibility for abusive behavior • saying
she caused it.

PHYSICAL VIOLENCE SEXUAL

ELLEN PENSE, FOUNDER OF THE DOMESTIC ABUSE INTERVENTION PROJECT IN DULUTH, MINNESOTA, DEVELOPED THE POWER AND CONTROL WHEEL, PICTURED HERE, TO DESCRIBE METHODS USED BY ABUSERS IN DOMESTIC VIOLENCE.

gets angry with his partner in a grocery store or other public place, he waits until they are in private to abuse her. According to the LAWC, research also shows that men who physically abuse women inflict blows in areas of the woman's body that are usually covered by clothes. This

THIS WOMAN STANDS AMID HUNDREDS OF PAIRS OF SHOES THAT WERE PLACED ON THE STEPS OF THE CAPITOL IN FRANKFORT, KENTUCKY, DURING A RALLY TO INCREASE PUBLIC AWARENESS OF DOMESTIC VIOLENCE.

behavior strongly suggests that men are in total control of their anger, not out of control. They plan every episode of violence.

What domestic violence is really about is power and control. The LAWC article mentioned here tells of a model of domestic violence proposed by Ellen Pense, founder of the Domestic Abuse Intervention Project in Duluth, Minnesota. This model, which is based on what

Pense calls a power and control wheel, describes the tactics that abusers use to exercise control over their intimate partners. Abusers shift or change tactics depending on what mood they are in, what the situation of the abuse is, and how their victims respond to the abuse. The model also suggests that abusers employ these tactics not only to control their partners but also to establish a relationship they can rely on in the future. In other words, abusers use various tactics to "train" their partners to give the responses they desire. Once the victim is trained, the abuser uses the same tactics over and over to reinforce the lesson.

Public Awareness of Domestic Violence

Until the early 1970s, domestic violence was not widely recognized in the United States. It wasn't until members of

Domestic violence reports constitute one-half of all violent crimes called to police departments. Mandatory arrest laws in twenty-four states require police to arrest all perpetrators of domestic violence.

the feminist movement, and battered women themselves, began to develop shelters for abused women that the issue was brought to the attention of the American public. Even today, only about half of domestic violence incidents are reported to the police. Victims of domestic violence give many reasons for not reporting their situations. Brittney Nichols, a clinical psychologist and a victims' advocate at the East Texas Crisis Center in Tyler, Texas, took a survey of domestic violence victims with whom she worked. The survey showed that almost half of the victims did not report the incidents of violence because they believed nothing could or would be done about them.

Some women were afraid to report the violence because they were in the country illegally or their abusers held their documents of legal residence. To control them, abusers told these women they would be deported if they reported being abused. However, deportation cannot happen in these cases. Law enforcement officers do not request residency status documents when they respond to domestic violence complaints. Immigration law requires that a woman be protected from domestic violence regardless of her residency status. Almost all the women who answered the survey were afraid their intimate partners would become more dangerous if they reported the abuse.

The Feminist Majority Foundation, an organization that works for women's equality, reproductive health, and nonviolence, says that women may be justified in failing to report domestic violence to the police. Many police departments do not have clear-cut procedures for handling domestic violence cases and fail to adequately document the extent of violence with photographs or other technical means. Even if arrested for assault, few men are prosecuted or convicted. Those that are convicted spend very little time in jail.

Lieutenant Richard Davis, a retired Brockton, Massachusetts, police officer and author of "Mandatory Arrest: A Flawed Policy Based on a False Premise," reports

Is someone hurting you? You can talk to me about it

VICTIMS OF VIOLENCE ARE OFTEN AFRAID TO TALK WITH OTHERS ABOUT THEIR PROBLEMS. BUTTONS LIKE THESE, WORN BY EMERGENCY ROOM PERSONNEL AND OTHERS WORKING WITH VICTIMS OF ABUSE, ENCOURAGE DISCLOSURE.

that mandatory arrest laws exist in twenty-four states. The remaining twenty-six states have preferred or pro-arrest laws that are similar to mandatory arrest laws. These laws require police officers to arrest all perpetrators of domestic violence regardless of what the act of violence is. A man who shoves his wife is as much at risk for being arrested as a man who viciously beats his wife.

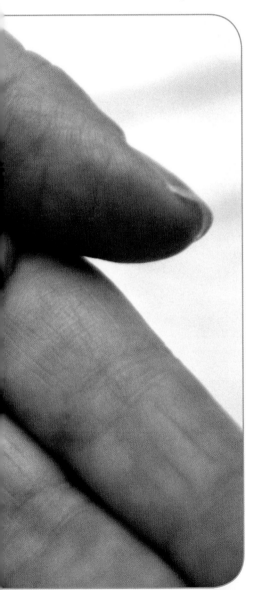

Many people dealing with victims of domestic violence applauded passage of these laws. They felt that victims of domestic violence were being ignored when they reported that they were being abused. If ignored, the victims were at risk for severe injury or even death in subsequent acts of domestic violence. Davis believes that these laws are based on the false idea that most law enforcement officers do not care about domestic violence victims. He also points out that "one-size-fits-all" laws almost never accomplish what they were intended to do because of the variability among situations in which they are applied. He strongly suggests that mandatory arrest laws be reexamined to see if they are effective. If not, he believes they should be abolished.

An unexpected result of these laws has been an increase in the number of women arrested for domestic violence. When officers arrive at the scene of a domestic violence incident, they may decide that both partners are acting aggressively and arrest them both. They don't take into account who is primarily responsible for the violence and who is acting in self-defense. Fortunately, many states are now developing policies and guidelines to help officers determine who the primary aggressor is in a violent incident. A primary aggressor is the person determined to be the most significant aggressor rather than the first person to act aggressively. In most cases, the man is the primary aggressor and the woman is defending herself and, all too often, her children. These guidelines may decrease the number of women being unjustifiably arrested in these situations.

ESCAPING FROM DOMESTIC VIOLENCE

Leaving an abuser can be dangerous. Because most men and boys use the tactics of domestic violence to maintain power and control over their intimate partners, they consider separation or breaking up as a loss of power. It is important that both girls and women seek advice and help as soon as they decide to leave an abusive relationship. In an article in *Maclean's* magazine entitled "Breakup Blast: Rejection Can Trigger a Brain 'Primed to Do Something

Her with her homework,
feel good about herself,
understand *consent* and *respect*.

...lk about sexual violence before it happens.

...e 16 Programs of the Vermont Network Against Domestic and Sexual Violence
...have been providing crisis services and education about what we can do when we
witness or experience sexual and domestic violence for over 20 years.
Help is available. Call for information and volunteer opportunities.

...-800-489-7273
...4/7 in Vermont   (489-RAPE)

Or Locally:

ESCAPING FROM ABUSIVE RELATIONSHIPS CAN BE DANGEROUS. BOTH
FEDERAL AND STATE PROGRAMS, LIKE THE VERMONT NETWORK
FEATURED HERE, ARE AVAILABLE TO HELP GIRLS AND WOMEN
CAUGHT IN THE WEB OF VIOLENCE.

Dangerous,'" Celia Milne reports on a study by Helen Fisher, a professor of anthropology at Rutgers University in New Jersey. Fisher has shown in her study that men are most dangerous shortly after the breakup of a relationship. They have lost control and have been rejected by the person whom they most want to control. It is in the immediate days and weeks after a breakup that most domestic murders occur. A few steps to take to improve the odds of safely escaping from domestic abuse include the following:

- Girls should talk to their mothers or other responsible adults who can help them seek protection. They should choose safe places to have these conversations and should not use cell phones or text messaging to do so. Abusive boyfriends can monitor phones and computers.
- Girls or women who feel they are in immediate danger should call 911 and report the situation to the police.
- If injured, a girl or woman should go to a local hospital emergency room for treatment and protection.
- If a girl or woman is unsure of what to do, she should call the National Domestic Violence Hotline. Volunteers are available to provide the phone numbers of local domestic violence shelters and other resources.
- The number one priority for both girls and women is to go somewhere that is safe. A safe house or women's shelter would be best. Not

only are shelters safe, but they are also good places to get information about legal aid, counseling, and other services. Some shelters also provide the means to evaluate and monitor the abusive partner.

Rebecca J. Burns, a domestic violence survivor, says, on the Web site http://thelaststraw.wordpress.com, "When I am asked why a woman doesn't leave [an] abuser, I say women stay because the fear of leaving is greater than the fear of staying. They will leave when the fear of staying is greater than the fear of leaving. At least this was true for me."

CHAPTER 2

Sexual Violence

Sexual violence occurs when a person of either sex forces some type of sexual attention or contact on a girl or woman against her will. There are many types of sexual violence, but they can be placed in three broad categories: visual sexual violence, verbal sexual violence, and physical sexual violence. Both visual and verbal sexual violence often precede physical sexual violence. A good example of verbal and visual sexual abuse preceding physical abuse occurs in stalking. Stalking involves intentional and repeated episodes of following, watching, calling, e-mailing, text messaging, and other types of harassment that are intended to create fear in the person being stalked. Stalking is an extreme form of psychological abuse. Daniel O'Leary, distinguished professor of psychology at the State University of New York at Stony Brook, in an article published in the journal *Violence and Victims*, says that psychological abuse almost always precedes physical abuse. Many victims of physical sexual assault are stalked before being attacked.

STALKING INVOLVES INTENTIONAL AND REPEATED EPISODES OF WATCHING AND FOLLOWING. IT IS A FORM OF PSYCHOLOGICAL SEXUAL ABUSE AND OFTEN PRECEDES PHYSICAL SEXUAL ABUSE.

TYPES OF SEXUAL VIOLENCE

Visual sexual violence includes voyeurism and exhibitionism. Voyeurism is a type of sexual violence where a man gets sexual gratification from watching a woman in some intimate activity when she believes she is alone. For instance, a voyeur, who in slang terms is called a "peeping Tom," may stand outside an incompletely covered window and watch a woman undress or take a bath. Watching pornographic movies or looking at magazines or Web sites that show explicit sexual acts are also forms of voyeurism.

Exhibitionism is another form of visual sexual violence. This occurs when a man purposefully exposes his genitals in a public place. The man gets sexual gratification from the reactions of women who don't expect to see private parts in public places.

Verbal sexual violence occurs when a man verbally threatens to sexually abuse a woman. Obscene phone calls are examples of verbal sexual abuse. In this cyberage, e-mail and text messages of a sexually explicit nature can also be considered verbal sexual abuse. This type of violence is very common. Abusers find it easier to violate their victims from afar than if the victims are present in person. Verbal sexual violence occurs when teens, often on a dare, randomly call a girl with whom they are not acquainted and "do a little trash talk." It also occurs when rappers or singers use sexually explicit language in their songs, or actors in movies and on television speak about violent sexual acts.

Physical sexual violence also takes many forms, including unwanted touching and sexual assault. Unwanted touching is sometimes called groping. The word "grope" means "to search out by feeling" but is frequently used in American slang to mean unwanted touching, fondling, or pinching of female breasts or genital areas. Groping occurs at unexpected times and in unexpected places. It often happens in crowded spaces such as in subways or elevators, or in the crush at sporting events or rock concerts. Regardless of where it happens, it is demeaning and a form of sexual violence.

Sexual assault is the ultimate form of sexual violence. Sexual assault includes rape, attempted rape, and other violent crimes that fall short of rape. The legal definition of rape is illegal bodily knowledge of a woman without her consent.

Rape: Vulnerability Factors

It is believed that most victims of sexual assault are girls and women. Boys and men can also be victims of sexual assault, but most of these cases are unreported. In a National Institute of Justice research report, Patricia Tzaden and Nancy Thoennes discuss what they call vulnerability factors for victimization. Several of the factors that make girls and women vulnerable to sexual assault include the following:

- Being female. It is thought that three-quarters of all rape victims are female.

(continued on page 36)

THAT'S NOT COOL CAMPAIGN FIGHTS DIGITAL DATING VIOLENCE

In January 2009, three Pennsylvania high school girls were charged with disseminating child pornography after they sent nude photographs of themselves, which they had taken with their cell phones, to their boyfriends. The boys were charged with possessing child pornography after receiving the pictures on their phones. Stephanie Clifford, a correspondent for the *New York Times*, wrote that this behavior is not unusual in today's teen cyberworld. As many as 20 percent of teens have been reported to have done the same thing. This is just one of many activities that teens do that are classified in the Family Violence Prevention Fund's category of digital dating violence. Others include sending nonstop text messages or posting cruel comments on Facebook or MySpace pages.

Alarmed by teens' use of digital technology to perpetrate violence, the Ad Council, a leading producer of public service advertisements that address the most pressing issues of the day, in partnership with the Family Violence Prevention Fund, launched a public service ad campaign and established a Web site called http://www.

THE TOP
Textual Harassm
Communicating Cle
Pic Pres
Constant Messag
Privacy Probl
Rumors Rur
Friend Needs

THIS PICTURE SHOWS THE "TALK IT OUT" PAGE OF THATSNOTCOOL.COM (HTTP://WWW.THATSNOTCOOL.COM). IT PROVIDES ONLINE COUNSELING AS WELL AS CHAT GROUPS TO DISCUSS "TEXTUAL VIOLENCE."

thatsnotcool.com in February 2009. Both the campaign and information available through the Web site encourage preadolescents and teens to talk online with trained volunteers to learn about digital violence and what they can do to stop it. The goal is to help teens set their own boundaries and to learn to tell their friends if they cross the line into "textual violence."

- Being young. More than half of all rape victims are less than eighteen years of age and 22 percent are twelve or younger.
- Being more trusting. Very often the abuser is someone trusted by the victim.
- Being poor. Poverty makes girls and women vulnerable to sexual assault by making it difficult for them to support themselves financially. They

SUSAN JONES, HERSELF A VICTIM OF ABUSE, OPERATES A WOMEN'S SHELTER IN ALASKA. A THIRD OF ALL AMERICAN RAPE VICTIMS ARE NATIVE AMERICAN WOMEN, INCLUDING THOSE IN ALASKA.

may be forced to depend on men, who may abuse them, for financial support. They may also be forced to engage in high-risk survival activities, such as trading sex for food, money, or other items. They are also likely to live in slums, where violence is more common than in better neighborhoods.

- Being a Native American. Almost a third of all rape victims in the United States are Native American women, including Alaskan native women. The incidence of rape of girls and women in other ethic groups is lower. Fifteen percent to 19 percent of African American, Latina, Asian, and Caucasian girls and women are victims of rape.

- Being the victim of previous sexual violence. Women who were assaulted as girls are two times more likely to be assaulted as adults than are women who were not victims of sexual assault in childhood.

- Being sexually promiscuous (undiscriminating or loose). Women and girls who have many sexual partners, especially those who practice unsafe sex, are very vulnerable to sexual abuse.
- Being drunk or drugged-out. Both alcohol and drugs make girls and women more vulnerable to sexual assault. The use of drugs and alcohol inhibits a person's judgment and frequently results in highly risky behavior.

Miriam Kaufman, an author and pediatrician working at the Hospital for Sick Children in Toronto, Canada, adds having disabilities to these vulnerability factors. Writing for the Committee on Adolescence of the American Academy of Pediatrics, Kaufman reports that children and teens with disabilities are twice as likely to be sexually assaulted as are those who aren't disabled. The most vulnerable are young girls and teens with milder cognitive disabilities. Cognition involves thinking, reasoning, and problem solving. People with cognitive disabilities may be unable to do any of these skills well. These girls are very easy to abuse because they are especially trusting and obedient.

TEENAGE GIRLS WHO HAVE BEEN RAPED OFTEN DEVELOP SEVERE DEPRESSION AS WELL AS SELF-DESTRUCTIVE BEHAVIORS SUCH AS SELF-MUTILATION, EATING DISORDERS, AND DRUG ABUSE.

THE CONSEQUENCES OF RAPE

Change is the consequence of rape. The life of a victim of rape is changed from the minute she is raped. The Centers for Disease Control and Prevention (CDC) reports that rape and other types of sexual assault can cause long-term health problems, including chronic pain, headaches, stomach trouble, and psychological and emotional problems. Women who have been raped are often fearful and anxious. They may never trust any man again. This can lead to a woman's being unable to form a meaningful relationship with a man and to marital problems.

Adolescent girls react to being raped somewhat differently from the way adult women react to being raped. In her article "Care of the Adolescent Sexual Assault Victim," in *Pediatrics*, Kaufman wrote that girls who have been raped are more likely than their peers who have not been raped to do the following:

- They have consensual (voluntary) sexual intercourse at a younger age.
- They practice unsafe sex, which may lead to pregnancy and the development of sexually transmitted diseases (STDs).
- They develop significant depression to the point of considering or attempting suicide.
- They develop self-harm behaviors, such as self-mutilation and eating disorders.
- They use alcohol and drugs.

STATUTORY RAPE AND TEEN PREGNANCY

Statutory rape is sexual intercourse with a person who is considered to be a minor. Jonna Spilbor, an attorney who is frequently a guest commentator on MSNBC and Court TV, says, "The idea behind statutory rape laws is that—in the eyes of the law—a person is incapable of consenting to various intimate acts until he or she reaches a certain age . . . States choose different, arbitrary numbers to approximate the age when they believe minors are mature enough to be able to meaningfully consent to sex." The age of consent in the various states ranges from twelve (in Oregon) to nineteen. Most states consider eighteen-year-olds to be capable of making adult decisions.

An article from the Community Crisis Center in Elgin, Illinois, reports that 70 percent of babies born to teenage mothers are fathered by adult men. Although as many as 20 percent of teen pregnancies result from forcible rape, many more result from statutory rape when a girl below the age of consent has consensual sexual intercourse with an adult male. Mireya Navarro, a New York Times correspondent, in "States Hope Statutory Rape Crackdown Will Fight Teen Pregnancy," says that by enforcing existing statutory rape laws and toughening others, authorities believe that most men will learn that girls are off limits. It is hoped that if men learn this lesson, the number of girls who find themselves pregnant and who must deal with the problems that arise from being teen mothers will plummet.

Both girls and women may develop what is called rape trauma syndrome. In the initial phase of this syndrome, which usually lasts from days to weeks, victims experience disbelief, anxiety, and fear. They are on an emotional roller-coaster ride—angry one minute and sad the next. All of this is mixed with unjustified feelings of guilt as they wonder if they were somehow responsible for the rape. The second phase of the syndrome is the outward adjustment phase in which a girl generally resumes her everyday activities. She still has not come to terms with the rape and may be significantly depressed. The reorganization phase is the third phase of the syndrome. This may last from months to years. During this phase, victims go through periods of adjustment and eventually reach some level of recovery. The level of recovery achieved is different for every victim of rape. Some authorities consider rape trauma syndrome to be a form of post-traumatic stress disorder (PTSD).

SEXUALLY TRANSMITTED DISEASES AND PREGNANCY AS CONSEQUENCES OF RAPE

Rape victims can develop sexually transmitted diseases (STDs) following rape, but many girls and women who are raped are already infected. A study published in the *New England Journal of Medicine* reported that as many as 45 percent of rape victims had STDs at the time they were raped. This number would be lower if only girls were considered because only about 50 percent of girls have had sexual intercourse before being raped.

Getting HIV is the main concern of most rape victims, although they are much more likely to get other types of STDs. The risk of getting HIV depends on how common it is in the community where the rape occurs and the nature of the rape. The likelihood that girls or women in the United

PREVEN®

Emergency Contraceptive Kit

(Levonorgestrel 0.25mg/Ethinyl Estradiol 0.05mg Tablet USP & Pregnancy Test)

- 1 Patient
- 1 Pregnan

TWENTY PERCENT OF TEEN PREGNANCIES RESULT FROM RAPE. MOST PREGNANCIES COULD BE AVOIDED IF TEENS SOUGHT MEDICAL HELP AND WERE GIVEN EMERGENCY CONTRACEPTION WITHIN SEVENTY-TWO HOURS OF THE RAPE.

States will get HIV after a single episode of rape is minimal. The likelihood of rape victims in African countries getting HIV, on the other hand, is much higher. Many men in Africa are HIV positive or have acquired immunodeficiency syndrome (AIDS). Certain drugs, if given to a rape victim within twenty-four hours after the rape, will minimize the risk of contracting HIV by as much as 80 percent. There are few rape crisis centers in Africa to distribute drugs to help prevent abused women from getting HIV and little money to pay for them. Girls who are victims of rape in the United States do have access to these drugs, however. If a girl or woman is raped by a man with AIDS, one who is known to be HIV positive, or one who injects drugs, she should consider taking a course of the medications. Emergency room and rape crisis center personnel, as well as a personal physician, can help victims make decisions about treatment options if they are at high risk for getting HIV.

Pregnancy is also a possible consequence of rape. Valerie Ulene is a physician who specializes in preventive medicine and who writes extensively on medical subjects for the Los Angeles Times. In her article "For Many Rape Victims, Treatment and Support Services Fall Short," Ulene says that the risk of pregnancy resulting from one act of sexual intercourse where no contraceptive measures are used ranges from 1 percent to 5 percent. The Rape, Abuse, and Incest National Network (RAINN) reports that in 2005, there were 64,800 completed rapes reported in the United States. So in that year, 3,240 pregnancies could have resulted from rape. The actual number is not known. Reports from both the

Community Crisis Center and from Malika Saada Saar, the executive director of the Rebecca Project for Human Rights, say that as many as 20 percent of teen pregnancies result from rape. Again, the actual number is not known.

Ulene points out that regardless of what the number of pregnancies resulting from rape really is, it could be reduced if all rape victims were adequately cared for in health care facilities. Just as there are drugs that can lessen the risk of contracting HIV after rape, there are also medications that can almost completely eliminate the risk of pregnancy after a rape. Emergency contraceptive pills, sometimes called "morning after" pills, if taken within seventy-two hours of unprotected intercourse, are 75 percent to 89 percent effective in preventing conception and pregnancy. Women, and especially teen girls, need to be educated about these drugs so that they will seek medical attention to obtain them if they are raped. This may help them avoid the potential risk of an unwanted pregnancy.

FALSE ACCUSATIONS OF RAPE

Just as rape itself is a devastating crime, falsely reporting a rape can be devastating for the man accused. Wendy McElroy, an author and a frequent columnist for FOX News, says that the topic of "bearing false witness" about rape creates many arguments between ardent feminists and groups who think that feminists are not being realistic. Feminists place the number of false reports of rape at about 2 percent. They contend that rape is so devastating and shame-provoking that most girls and women do not want anyone to know that they have been raped. Reports by others, including some law enforcement personnel and prosecutors, say that as many as 40 percent of accusations of rape are false. McElroy feels that both numbers are out of line—one much too low and the other much too high. Based on information from the Federal Bureau of Investigation (FBI) and from the Innocence Project, both of which report data supported by advanced technology, McElroy believes the actual number is closer to 20 percent. The Innocence Project is a national public policy organization founded by two prominent attorneys. The goal of the project is to use scientific technology, including DNA testing, to exonerate people who have been wrongfully imprisoned for crimes they did not commit. To date, 227 men have been released from prison, some of whom were wrongfully convicted of rape.

When asked why a woman would falsely accuse a man of rape, Joseph Carver, a clinical psychologist, gave the following reasons:

LARRY FULLER *(CENTER)*, SEEN HERE WITH TWO INNOCENCE PROJECT LAWYERS, WAS FREED, BASED ON DNA EVIDENCE, AFTER SERVING TWENTY-FIVE YEARS IN PRISON FOR A RAPE HE DID NOT COMMIT.

- To get revenge. False accusation is an extreme way to punish someone.
- To break up a relationship. A daughter might accuse her stepfather of raping her to break up his marriage with her mother.
- To gain legal advantage. False accusation of rape or sexual abuse is often used in court to

47

gain legal advantage in child custody cases during divorce actions.

- To get attention. This is an extreme attention-seeking strategy seen in individuals with personality or mental health problems.
- To deflect responsibility. A pregnant teenager might accuse a man of rape rather than admit to her parents that she's sexually active.

Karen Stephenson summed up the issue in her article "False Allegations." She said, "When men are falsely accused of rape, they become a victim of rape."

MYTHS and Facts

MYTH
Domestic violence is usually a one-time isolated occurrence.

Fact
Domestic violence is characterized by repeated episodes of abuse.

MYTH
Girls and women entice men to rape.

Fact
Rape is the responsibility of the rapist alone. It is not the fault of the victim. Most rapes are planned. The rapist only waits for an appropriate opportunity and place to execute his plan.

MYTH
Few date rapes are "enabled" by the use of alcohol and drugs.

Fact
Alcohol and drug use before date rape is reported by more than 40 percent of teen victims of date rape and the same number of teen rapists.

CHAPTER 3

DATE VIOLENCE

Date violence occurs when a girl or woman is emotionally, psychologically, or physically harmed by a dating partner. It is the most common type of violence against teen girls. Elaine Landau, in her book *Date Violence*, writes that the notion of abusive teen relationships is relatively new but that violence among dating teens is as common as it is in adult marriages. About 20 percent of all adolescents claim to have experienced either psychological or physical violence from a dating partner. It is often difficult to recognize the early signs of date violence but it is important to do so because they may be preludes to physical violence. A girl should be wary of a dating partner if he does one or more of the following things:

- If he makes fun of her or intentionally humiliates her in front of friends.
- If he says she is worthless and without merit.

CONSTANT TEXT MESSAGING BY A DATING PARTNER MAY BE
FLATTERING EARLY IN A RELATIONSHIP. IT CAN, HOWEVER, BECOME A
MEANS OF PSYCHOLOGICAL CONTROL AND CAN BE A FORERUNNER
OF DATING VIOLENCE.

- If he blames her for his bad feelings and mistakes.
- If he criticizes all of her decisions and views.
- If he belittles or makes light of her hopes, dreams, and achievements.
- If he incessantly text messages or phones her many times throughout the day and night.
- If he constantly tries to convince her to have sex and uses guilt to do so.

Physical violence among dating couples is the same as that inflicted in domestic violence. It includes restraining, pinching, kicking, choking, pushing, shoving, slapping, biting, burning, hair pulling, and sexual assault, among other actions. Sexual assault in the setting of date violence is any type of sexual activity that is forced on a girl by her dating partner. It includes rape and attempted rape.

DATE RAPE

Date rape, also called acquaintance rape, is rape that occurs between two people who are dating or who know each other. Mike Hardcastle, a special needs foster parent, youth adviser, and author, in "What Every Guy Must Know About Date Rape," says, "Call it date rape, call it acquaintance rape, or just call it what it is, rape; whatever you call it, it's a crime and it is committed at a shocking rate of every two minutes in North America." Yes, date rape is rape, but it is different from rape by a stranger in several ways.

♀ PREVENT RAPE

Rape has nothing to do with passion or love. Rape is a crime of power and control that one in six women in the United States will experience in her lifetime. Rape victims range in age from young infants to the elderly. According to the Rape, Abuse, and Incest National Network (RAINN), 15 percent of rape victims are under the age of twelve. Girls who are ages sixteen to nineteen are four times more likely than the general population of women to be victims of rape.

Although not addressing rape specifically, Henry de Bracton, a British judge, in his book *On the Laws and Customs of England*, written in 1240, noted, "An ounce of prevention is worth a pound of cure." That says it all when it comes to rape. It is far better to prevent rape than to have to deal with its consequences. Here are a few recommendations from the American Academy of Pediatrics to help girls avoid being raped:

- Don't attend parties given by unknown people.
- Don't meet with people known only from Internet contacts.
- Don't walk alone at night.
- Don't pose for nude or sexually explicit photographs.
- Don't use drugs of any kind.
- Don't drink from anything that has been left unattended.
- Don't accept drinks from a stranger.
- Do go to parties with a "buddy" and stay in touch with that friend.

Perhaps the most significant of these differences is that girls are more vulnerable to date rape than to rape by a stranger. It is hard for a girl to believe that a guy she really likes and has admired can be a rapist. Scott Linquist, a rape prevention specialist, reports that 84 percent of all rapes are date or acquaintance rapes. In his book *The Date Rape*

Prevention Book, Linquist says that girls and women are especially vulnerable to rape by men they know. They are taught to be wary of strangers, but they let down their guards with dates, friends, and acquaintances.

When a girl is raped by a stranger, she is often beaten and otherwise injured as well as being raped. In date

rape, such violence is less common, although it can occur. Even though a girl has no bruises or other physical injuries, if she is penetrated in any way, she has been raped. Rape victims, especially date rape victims, may find that they can never trust men again. Far beyond the physical trauma of rape, the loss of trust may be the most significant consequence of rape.

ALCOHOL, DRUGS, AND DATE RAPE

Alcohol and drugs are major factors in date rape. Linquist calls them rape enablers. In spite of recent media

THESE CALIFORNIA WOMEN TEST THEIR DRINKS FOR DATE RAPE DRUGS USING DRINK COASTERS. LAW ENFORCEMENT EXPERTS BELIEVE THAT "TEST COASTERS" ARE INEFFECTIVE, WHILE MANUFACTURERS CLAIM THEY ARE 95 PERCENT ACCURATE.

coverage about date rape drugs, alcohol is still the major enabler of date rape. Most people think that alcohol is a stimulant because they initially feel better when they use it. The "lift" people feel with its use is really a loss of inhibitions rather than stimulation. Alcohol is actually a depressant. In large enough quantities, it causes people to get sleepy. It also decreases male sexual performance. That is why most men with date rape in mind tend to minimize their own alcohol consumption. They furnish their dates with lots of alcohol while drinking little themselves. Sooner or later a girl will fail to say no or may become incapable of saying no. At that point, sexual intercourse becomes rape.

Drugs such as marijuana and cocaine have been enablers of date rape for years. There are three drugs, however, that are specifically known as date rape drugs. These are Rohypnol (the brand name for flunitrazepam), GHB, and ketamine. The street names for Rohypnol include roofies, ruffies, roche, R2, Mexican valium, rib, and rope, among others. It is a medication usually prescribed as a sleeping pill in Europe and Latin America. It is illegal in the United States. It is a white tablet that dissolves quickly in liquids. It adds no taste, color, or odor to beverages. Besides causing drowsiness and loss of inhibitions and judgment, it can also cause amnesia.

GHB is gamma hydroxybutyrate. It is also called grievous bodily harm or liquid ecstasy. GHB was originally developed as an anesthetic to put people to sleep before surgical procedures. It causes unconsciousness and amnesia, qualities that make it a perfect date rape drug. Unfortunately, it can also cause life-threatening symptoms, such as reduced heart rate, seizures, and respiratory failure. It is particularly dangerous when used with alcohol. GHB comes in a liquid form, so it can easily be added to a date's drink.

Ketamine, also called special K and super K, was originally produced to be used as an anesthetic for people and by veterinarians working with large animals. It can be obtained legally by prescription for those purposes. Among its side effects are confusion, lack of coordination, and amnesia in those recovering from its use. Ketamine is also extremely dangerous when used with alcohol.

ARE YOU A VICTIM OF DATE RAPE DRUGS?

Because victims of date rape in which date rape drugs were used may not remember the event, they may need to look for clues to determine if it really happened. An article on date rape drugs on http://teenadvice.about.com suggests looking for the following clues:

- A date rape victim may feel hungover despite having ingested little or no alcohol.
- A date rape victim may have a sense of having had a hallucination or a very "real" dream.

Victims of date rape drugs often feel hungover despite having ingested little or no alcohol.

LOVE PSYCHOLOGICAL human rights ABUSIVE BEHAVIORS
DOMESTIC POWER VIOLENCE STEREOTYPES dysfunctional
women

- A date rape victim may have fleeting memories of feeling or acting intoxicated although she did not use alcohol.
- A date rape victim may have no clear memory of events during an eight- to twenty-four-hour period.
- A date rape victim may be told stories by others about how intoxicated she seemed at a time when she knew she had not used alcohol or drugs.
- A date rape victim may experience pain and discomfort in her vagina.

A girl who strongly suspects she has been a victim of a date rape drug should go to a health care facility or to her personal physician as soon as possible. Blood tests may confirm the presence of remaining date rape drugs in her blood if her blood is drawn within twelve to twenty-four hours of the drug being ingested.

WHAT TO DO IF YOU ARE RAPED

Rape is a major trauma. It is experienced as a loss of control. Too often, it renders a girl or woman incapable of doing much of anything. That is one of the reasons rape is an underreported crime. Authorities on rape say that there are steps that a rape victim should and should not take. A few of these actions are listed below.

- She should get to a safe area as quickly as possible.

- She should go to a hospital emergency room to get a medical exam in which specimens are collected that can help to identify the rapist.
- She should report the crime to the police, school authorities, campus police, or emergency medical personnel.
- She should call a trusted friend or family member for support during examinations.

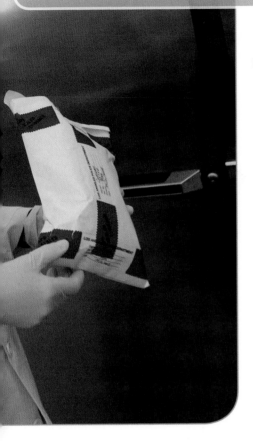

- She should contact a rape crisis center for understanding, support, and information.
- She should get counseling.

A rape victim should not do any of the following because she may destroy evidence needed to identify and convict her rapist:

- She should not shower, bathe, douche, or otherwise clean up before going to an emergency room or rape crisis center.
- She should not change clothes before going to an emergency room or rape crisis center.
- She should not straighten up the house or apartment if it was the scene of the rape.

Many rape victims consider it a sign of weakness to ask for help after they have been raped. To the contrary,

getting counseling is a healthy sign—one that says that a victim wants to take back control of her life. She wants to be a survivor of rape rather than a victim of it. To get the most help from counseling sessions, it is beneficial for a girl or woman to have questions in mind that she needs answered. (See the sample questions to ask a counselor on page 64.)

SEEKING COUNSELING IS AN EARLY STEP TOWARD RECOVERY FOR RAPE VICTIMS. MOST RAPE CRISIS CENTERS AND WOMEN'S SHELTERS PROVIDE COUNSELING OR CAN REFER RAPE VICTIMS TO APPROPRIATE COUNSELORS.

Benefits from counseling won't come in a day. Some girls and women find it takes only a session or two to get them headed on the road to acceptance and recovery from rape. Others take much longer. The important point is to stick with it until the counselor advises otherwise. There are many support groups that can also provide help for victims of rape who need friends who have "been there, done that."

Ten Great Questions
TO ASK A COUNSELOR

1.
Was the rape my fault?

2.
Did the way I dressed or acted lead to my rape?

3.
Will I be raped again?

4.
How can I protect myself in the future?

5.
Will I get HIV?

6.
Will I get pregnant?

7.
How can I learn to trust men again?

8.
If I report the rape, what will happen to the rapist?

9.
Are there any agencies that will help me pay for counseling?

10.
How can I help prevent other girls from being raped?

CHAPTER 4

Violence Against Women: War and Warriors

Before the early 1970s, domestic violence was practically unknown, although it had existed for centuries. Until the mid-1980s, date rape in high school circles and on college campuses was only discussed in hushed tones. Now these topics make newspaper headlines and television's prime-time news. During the last ten years of the twentieth century and the first years of the twenty-first century, increasing attention has been and is being focused on the problem of violence against women both by and within the U.S. military.

Violence Against Women by the U.S. Military

Conquering armies often believe that, as the victors, they are entitled to use and abuse the women of the clans, tribes, or countries that lose the war. Unfortunately, some

ABEER QASSIM HAMZA, AN IRAQI GIRL, WAS RAPED, MURDERED, AND INCINERATED AT THIS SITE IN HER HOME BY FIVE U.S. SOLDIERS. THEY ALSO KILLED HER PARENTS AND SISTER.

U.S. troops believe the same thing. Despite the efforts of military leaders to prevent it, some U.S. military personnel are still assaulting and raping local women in countries where the soldiers are stationed. Recent examples of this include sexual assaults on some of the girls and women in Iraq.

Ruth Rosen, a journalist and professor of history and public policy at the University of California, Berkeley, in "The Hidden War on Women in Iraq," wrote: "Iraqi women, like women everywhere, have always been vulnerable to rape." She reports that since the American invasion of Iraq, the problem has worsened. Women are literally disappearing from public life as they imprison themselves in their homes. It seems better to stay at home than to risk sexual assault by some American soldiers or kidnapping and abuse by uncontrolled local gangs. A specific example given by Rosen is the case of Abeer Qassim Hamza, a fourteen-year-old Iraqi girl who was raped and killed by five U.S. soldiers. Her body was set on fire to cover up the crime, and her parents and sister were murdered. Since the incident, three soldiers have pled guilty to rape and a fourth has been tried and convicted of rape. They received sentences ranging from twenty-seven months to one hundred years in military prisons. The fifth man, who was discharged from the military before details of the rape and murders were known, was tried in civilian court. He was found guilty of rape and of the murders and received a life sentence without parole. Many Iraqi citizens believe that none of these sentences was severe enough.

Incidents of sexual assault on women prisoners held at Abu Ghraib, a prison run by the U.S. military in Iraq, have been videotaped. These videos have been reviewed by military leaders and members of the U.S. Congress who are developing ways to crack down on violence against women by U.S. military personnel. The videos reportedly show multiple episodes of rape perpetrated by some American soldiers on Iraqi female prisoners. These incidents are just a few of the abuses allegedly committed by some U.S. troops in Iraq.

VIOLENCE AGAINST WOMEN WITHIN THE U.S. MILITARY

Diana Price, writing for the National Organization for Women (NOW), reported that in 2006 almost 15 percent of active duty military troops were women (that's about 202,248 women). In addition, there were 141,922

MORE THAN 200,000 WOMEN SERVE IN THE U.S. MILITARY. TWENTY-THREE PERCENT WILL EXPERIENCE SOME FORM OF SEXUAL ASSAULT BY THEIR COMRADES-IN-ARMS WHILE ON ACTIVE DUTY.

women in the reserves and 63,831 in the National Guard. About 60,000 female troops have been sent overseas to support the wars in Iraq and Afghanistan since those wars began. One in seven U.S. troops in Iraq is female.

Jake Willens, in "Women in the Military: Combat Roles Considered," points out that women have served in the U.S. military since the Revolutionary War. It was not until

President Harry Truman signed the Women's Armed Services Integration Act in 1948, however, that women gained professional military status. The act limited the number of women in the military to 2 percent of the total force and spelled out what military occupational specialties (MOS) women could fill. At the present time, women fill almost every MOS in the military with the exception of combat slots. One of the arguments used against women serving in combat positions is that if they become prisoners of war they are likely to be sexually abused by enemy forces.

Sadly, the greatest risk of sexual abuse for women in the military comes from their comrades-in-arms. In the 2008 Annual Report on Military Service Sexual Assault, prepared by the Department of Defense for Congress, it was reported that 2,900 sexual assaults had occurred among 1.4 million active military members in the year ending September 30, 2008. More than half of these assaults were rapes. In commenting on this report, Julia Ritchey, a correspondent for the Voice of America, said, "Defense Department officials acknowledge that the numbers are stark and that about 80 percent of rapes go unreported."

CAUSES OF VIOLENCE AGAINST MILITARY WOMEN

According to Helen Benedict, a professor of journalism at Columbia University in New York City who writes extensively on social justice and women, military women are raped twice as often as are their civilian counterparts. Benedict says that sexual violence persists in the military because of

VIGIL AT FORT BRAGG'S GATES

On October 8, 2008, a vigil was held at the gates of Fort Bragg, one of the U.S. Army's largest military bases. The vigil was held to commemorate the lives of four U.S military women who had been murdered in North Carolina in the nine months preceding the vigil. An editorial published in the Fayetteville, North Carolina, *Observer* said, "It's an old argument, we train men, and now women, to wage war, then we are baffled when they do that to each other . . . In a way it's surprising that there aren't more bodies piling up at military bases all over this nation." Although preventive measures are being taken by the military to stop violence against its women, they are obviously not enough. One of the purposes of the vigil, which was kept by forty men and women, was to call for renewed efforts to prevent further deaths. Ann Wright, a retired U.S. Army colonel and a former diplomat who resigned from the State Department in protest over the war in Iraq, in writing about the vigil for http://www.truthout.org said, "Sadly, no one from the Military Command Authority nor from the prevention of domestic violence offices at Fort Bragg made the effort to come to the gates to talk about ending the epidemic of violence."

a "confluence of military culture, the psychology of the assailants, and the nature of war." Military culture contributes misogyny, the hatred of women, to the equation. Benedict believes that misogyny "lies at the root of why soldiers rape." Men who enter the military, according to Benedict, are made to feel that they won't fit in unless they harass and belittle women whenever they can. It's the macho thing to do so even the "nicest guys" may find themselves assaulting women.

Several scholars whom Benedict mentions in her paper have investigated the psychology of assailants. These include criminologist Menachim Amir and psychologists Nicholas Groth and Gene Abel. The conclusions that these men drew from their separate studies were similar. They found that rapists are not motivated by lust but by a mixture of anger, sexual viciousness, and the need to dominate someone. Benedict also refers to work by Rutgers University law professor Elizabeth Hillman that suggests that today's all-volunteer army is attractive to men who are prone to rape because these men perceive that violence is acceptable in the military setting.

The nature of war also contributes to violence against women. Benedict says that Robert Lifton, distinguished professor of psychology and psychiatry at John Jay College in New York City, has studied and written extensively about war and war crimes. He believes that soldiers are particularly prone to commit atrocities in certain types of war. Wars that have no well-defined armies and that have been justified by

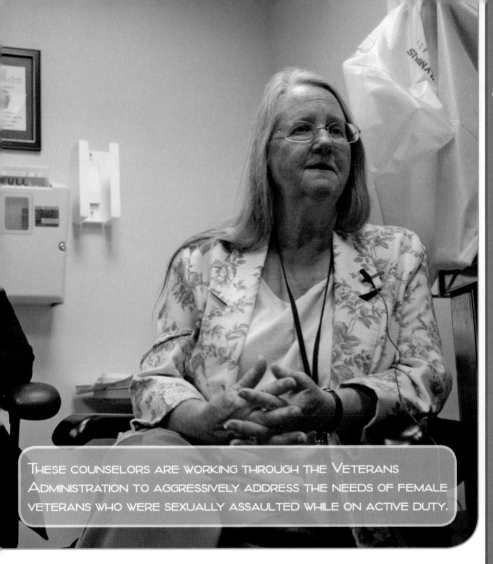

THESE COUNSELORS ARE WORKING THROUGH THE VETERANS ADMINISTRATION TO AGGRESSIVELY ADDRESS THE NEEDS OF FEMALE VETERANS WHO WERE SEXUALLY ASSAULTED WHILE ON ACTIVE DUTY.

false information are those in which many atrocities occur. It was difficult in the war in Vietnam and is equally challenging in the present wars in Iraq and Afghanistan for U.S. military personnel to identify the enemy. Enemy armies are not well defined. Some soldiers have a hard time justifying what they are ordered to do so they come to loathe themselves. They may express their self-hatred, as well as their fear and anger, by acting violently against those around them. Often, these are the military women with whom they serve.

TREATING VIOLENCE AGAINST WOMEN IN THE MILITARY

Several steps have been and continue to be taken to treat the victims of what is called military sexual trauma (MST) and to correct practices within the military that lead to it. Treatment of victims of MST usually falls to Veterans Affairs (VA) medical personnel because victims on active duty are very hesitant to report the crime for fear of retaliation and harassment by their male colleagues. They wait until they leave the military and then seek treatment. The aftereffects of sexual trauma, as reported by retired military women being cared for in VA medical facilities, include the following:

- They avoid places or objects that cause them to recall the traumatic incident.
- They frequently feel that something is missing or not right.
- They may abuse alcohol and drugs.
- They sometimes develop severe depression with suicidal thoughts.
- They have recurring and intrusive thoughts and dreams about the traumatic incident.
- They have many non-specific health problems.
- They develop relationship problems.

Since 2002, the VA has screened all (male and female) discharged military personnel for MST. Russell Goldman, a broadcast journalist, on an ABC News report, said that between 2002 and 2007, more than 62,000 female veterans stated that they had been subjected to uninvited sexual attention or had been sexually assaulted while on active duty. The VA is making structural changes in existing facilities and opening new facilities to specifically treat women with MST. These centers provide both inpatient and outpatient care and counseling to MST victims. In 2007, there were fifteen federally funded programs across the United States for this purpose and others were opened in 2008.

STOPPING VIOLENCE AGAINST WOMEN IN THE MILITARY

Stopping the violence is as important as treating MST. Many efforts have been made to do so, but the apparent increase in the numbers of cases reported would suggest that efforts have been inadequate. In March 2008, the Department of Defense released its fourth annual report on sexual assault in the military. An article by Amie Newman, managing editor for *RH Reality Check*, an online publication advancing sexual and reproductive health and rights, says that the report again showed an increase in the number of assaults on military women. She goes on to say that the U.S. House of Representatives Subcommittee on National Security and Foreign Affairs held a hearing on sexual assault in the military on July 31, 2008. Representative Louise Slaughter of New York reintroduced a bill called the Military Domestic and Sexual Violence Response Act that, if passed, will establish an Office of Victims Advocate

I. A.M. STRONG

INTERVENE ★ ACT ★ MOTIVATE

Sexual Assault and Sexual Harassment Prevention

INTERVE

When I recognize a threat to my fellow Soldiers, I will
the personal courage to **INTERVENE** and prevent Se
Assault. I will condemn acts of Sexual Harassment.
not abide obscene gestures, language or beha
I am a Warrior and a member of a t
I will **INTER**

A

You are my brother, my sister, my fellow So
It is my duty to stand up for you, no matter the
or place. I will take **ACTION**. I will do what's
I will prevent Sexual Harassment and Ass
I will not tolerate sexually offensive beha
I will

MOTIVA

We are American Soldiers, **MOTIVAT**
keep our fellow Soldiers safe. It is
mission to prevent Sexual Harassr
and Assault. We will denounce se
misconduct. As Soldiers, we a
MOTIVATED to take ac
We are strongest...toge

www.preventsexualassault.army.mil
Military OneSource • 1-800-342-9647

I. A.M. STRONG IS A U.S. ARMY SEXUAL ASSAULT PREVENTION AND
RESPONSE PROGRAM THAT CALLS ON SOLDIERS TO INTERVENE IF
THEY OBSERVE SEXUALLY ABUSIVE BEHAVIOR AMONG COLLEAGUES.

(OVA) within the Department of Defense. It would also strengthen policies for reporting, prosecuting, and treating perpetrators, and would expand counseling and treatment programs for victims through the VA.

The army has instituted a new program known as "I. A.M. Strong" (the words "I Am" stand for "intervene, act, motivate"), which calls for soldiers to confront peers who are abusing alcohol or are participating in other behaviors that could lead to sexual assault. Soldiers are expected to alert higher-ranking personnel if their colleagues' behavior does not improve. In an article in the *Wall Street Journal*, correspondent Yochi Dreazen discussed the I. A.M. Strong program. He says that skeptics believe that this program is unlikely to work, as similar programs have failed in the past. Most critics believe that the military's effort to combat sexual violence has been hampered by a lack of support from some senior commanders. Joseph Biden, vice president of the United States, has been a strong advocate for women's rights. As a U.S. senator, he not only wrote and introduced the Violence Against Women Act (VAWA), which was adopted by the U.S. Congress in 1994, but also wrote the International Violence Against Women Act and presented it to Congress in 2007. The act is a historic and unprecedented effort by the United States to address violence against women globally. Senior military commanders may find that more emphasis is placed on stopping violence against women in the military under the leadership of President Barack Obama and Vice President Biden than it was in previous administrations.

CHAPTER 5

STOPPING VIOLENCE AGAINST WOMEN

As previously documented in this book, violence against women is as old as humankind itself. It is based on patriarchal cultural beliefs that men "rule the roost" and have the right to use and abuse girls and women as they see fit. It is based on the need of many men to exert power and control over women to demonstrate their masculinity. In some cases, it is based on misogyny. Violence against women is considered, in both the United States and internationally, to be one of today's greatest public health issues for women. The CDC reports that the health-related costs of rape, physical assault, stalking, and domestic homicide are $5.8 billion each year. The question is, what is being done to stop the violence?

FEDERAL EFFORTS TO STOP VIOLENCE AGAINST WOMEN

Prior to 1990, there were many U.S. Codes (laws), including the Victims of Crime Act (VOCA) of 1984, addressing violent acts in general. Congress passed the VOCA because of the explosion of violence in the United States during the 1970s and early 1980s. In 1990, additional legislation was introduced in Congress to supplement the VOCA. At the same time, Representative Pat Schroeder of Colorado and Senator Joseph Biden of Delaware introduced legislation in the House and Senate to specifically address issues of violence against women. Congress passed the Violence Against Women Act (VAWA) in August 1994, as part of the Violent Crime Control and Law Enforcement Act.

The VAWA was considered by most authorities to be a vital first step in America's efforts to recognize and treat violence against women as a serious problem. In explaining the provisions of the act, experts at the Family Violence Prevention Fund say that the act made domestic violence and sexual assault crimes punishable by law. It also provided funding for several programs to encourage states to address domestic violence and sexual assault. Other grants were given to educate police, other law enforcement personnel, and prosecutors about violence against girls and women. Emphasis was placed on the need to treat victims as victims, not as perpetrators. Diana Russell, professor emeritus of sociology at Mills College in Oakland, California, and one of the world's foremost experts on sexual violence against women, in her book *The Politics of Rape*, gives an example of this need. A woman that she interviewed while writing her book said, "When a person is robbed, the robber is put on trial. When someone is murdered, the murderer is tried. But

SENATOR JOSEPH BIDEN OF DELAWARE, ALONG WITH
REPRESENTATIVE PATRICIA SCHROEDER OF COLORADO (SECOND
FROM RIGHT) SPEAK ABOUT THE VIOLENCE AGAINST WOMEN ACT
(VAWA), WHICH WAS PASSED BY THE U.S. CONGRESS IN 1994.

when a woman is raped, it is the woman and not the rapist who is put on trial."

The VAWA also established the Office of Violence Against Women within the U.S. Department of Justice and authorized and funded a National Domestic Violence Hotline. Congress reauthorized the act in both 2000 and 2005. It will need to be reauthorized again in 2010 if its programs are to be funded.

Congress passed a second piece of legislation to fight violence against women in 2004 and reauthorized it in 2008. It is called the Debbie Smith Act. With advancement in the technology to analyze DNA (deoxyribonucleic acid), law enforcement officials and courts were given tools that they had not previously had to solve rape cases. DNA is the material in body cells that carry a person's genetic code (genome). No two people have exactly the same genetic code. If a woman is raped and semen or other material (such as a hair or skin cells) from the rapist can be obtained, he can be identified by analyzing the DNA in these samples. In 2004, Congress passed the Debbie Smith Act to provide funding to process the DNA from thousands of unsolved cases of rape that were and still are backlogged in state and local crime laboratories. The processing of backlogged DNA samples has benefited some men as well. Several men who were accused, convicted, and imprisoned for rape have been

THE VAWA ESTABLISHED THE OFFICE ON VIOLENCE AGAINST WOMEN IN THE U.S. DEPARTMENT OF JUSTICE AND PROVIDED FUNDING FOR THE NATIONAL DOMESTIC VIOLENCE HOTLINE (800-799-7233), WHOSE WEB SITE IS SHOWN HERE (HTTP://WWW.NDVH.ORG).

found to be innocent, based on DNA analysis, and have been freed from prison.

EDUCATIONAL EFFORTS TO STOP VIOLENCE

Following several episodes of violence in which girls were injured or killed by former boyfriends while at school, educators are stepping up to try to stem the violence. Elizabeth Olson, a correspondent for the *New York Times*, in "Killings Prompt Efforts to Spot and Reduce Abuse of Teenagers in Dating," reports on several programs now under way. She says that Texas has recently adopted a law that requires school districts to define dating violence in school safety codes. This was prompted by the stabbing death of Ortralla Mosley, a fifteen-year-old, in a hallway of an Austin, Texas, high school and the shooting death of Jennifer Ann Crecente, an eighteen-year-old.

Also mentioned in this article is the Lindsay Ann Burke Act, which was passed by the Rhode Island legislature in October 2008. This act requires all middle and high school students in Rhode Island to take educational programs to learn about the widespread dangers of dating violence. Lindsay Ann Burke was a twenty-three-year-old who was murdered by an abusive former boyfriend. Her mother, Ann Burke, teaches health classes in a Rhode Island middle school. She helped to push this act through the legislature and has developed programs to educate teachers about the subject. Although the programs will vary from school to school, all will be aimed at helping students to appreciate the extent of and dangers of dating violence.

TEENS FIGHTING VIOLENCE AGAINST GIRLS AND WOMEN

Violence against girls and women is an epidemic that is difficult to treat. Like almost any epidemic, it is far better to prevent it than to try to treat it. The most important step in

A Georgia teen writes on a T-shirt during a Stop the Violence rally. She and many of her friends are working to stop the violence against girls and women.

preventing this epidemic is to educate young people and to get them involved in helping to stop the violence. Several outstanding programs have been developed by and for teens. Only a few of them are presented here. Each of them has the same goal—to stop the violence.

CORPORATIONS AND FOUNDATIONS FIGHTING VIOLENCE AGAINST WOMEN

On November 26, 2008, the Robert Woods Johnson Foundation announced eleven recipients for funding in a new program called Building Healthy Teen Relationships. According to a spokesperson for the Family Violence Prevention Fund, which is a partner in the program with the Robert Woods Johnson Foundation, eighteen million dollars are being invested by the foundation over four years to help prevent teen dating violence and sexual abuse. Most recipients of the funding are schools or health care facilities, each of which will receive about one million dollars to finance their programs. Each group will work with students in the sixth through eighth grades using older teens as mentors. The programs will, among other things, train older teens, teachers, coaches, and parents in methods to promote healthier teen relationships.

Since 1991, the clothing company Liz Claiborne, Inc., has been working to end domestic violence through its Love Is Not Abuse program. The program provides information and tools that men, women, children, teens, and corporate executives can use to learn more about the issue of domestic violence and how they can help end this epidemic.

The Avon Foundation also helps in the fight against domestic violence through its Speak Out Against Domestic Violence program. The Avon Foundation has contributed more than $580 million to stop domestic violence throughout the world.

Students Taking Action for Respect (STAR) began in 2001 because students in several Texas high schools realized how big a problem dating violence and sexual abuse had become. At that time, a survey showed that three out of four Texans between the ages of sixteen and twenty-four had experienced abuse in a dating relationship or knew someone who had. The STAR program, under the guidance of the Texas Association Against Sexual Assault (TAASA), provides youth with leadership skills and the knowledge to talk to their peers about the issues of dating violence and sexual abuse. There are now more than four hundred youth leaders throughout Texas who present programs on sexual and dating violence to their peers in schools and community groups. The program has reached more than 13,000 students in 130 communities so far.

Launched nationally in 2006, Choose Respect is a program developed by the Division of Violence Prevention of the CDC to help adolescents form healthy relationships to prevent dating abuse before it starts. The program is aimed at young people from eleven to fourteen years of age because they are still forming attitudes and beliefs that will affect how they are treated and how they treat others. Choose Respect publicizes its messages through eCards, posters, bookmarks, pocket guides, online games, television and radio programs, and other media.

On a Friday night in 1989, Alex Orange died trying to break up a fight at a party. His friends didn't just send flowers to his funeral, they also formed Students Against

Respect. Give it. Get it.
Play it at chooserespect.org

CHOOSE ▶ RESPECT

CDC

CHOOSE RESPECT IS A PROGRAM DEVELOPED BY THE CENTERS
FOR DISEASE CONTROL AND PREVENTION. ITS GOAL IS TO HELP
ELEVEN- TO FOURTEEN-YEAR-OLDS BUILD HEALTHY RELATIONSHIPS
TO PREVENT DATING VIOLENCE.

Violence Everywhere (SAVE). In the twenty years since this student-driven organization was formed, it has expanded its membership to 200,000 teens in more than 1,700 SAVE chapters across the United States. The various programs sponsored by SAVE teach teens that there are alternatives to violence and provide opportunities for them to practice what they learn through school and service projects. Dating violence is covered in the programs of this group.

Another bright spot in the fight to stop violence against women is the role that some men are taking to stop the violence. The Coaching Boys Into Men campaign is an example of one of the programs developed by men for men and boys. This program invites men to be part of the solution for stopping violence against girls and women by teaching boys that violence never equals strength. It is being cosponsored by the Family Violence Prevention Fund and the Waitt Institute for Violence Prevention. The institute is funded by the Waitt Family Foundation, which was formed by Ted Waitt, the founder of Gateway Computers. Before the program started, surveys showed that fewer than 29 percent of men talked to boys about violence against girls and women. Since 2000, the number of men who actively talk to boys about violence has increased significantly. A spokesperson for the Family Violence Prevention Fund says, "True progress toward ending violence against women and children will only be achieved when a critical mass of men are actively involved in the solution by talking to the boys in their lives."

HIP-HOP: BEYOND BEATS AND RHYMES

Byron Hurt was a young boy when hip-hop appeared in the Bronx, one of the boroughs of New York City. He is now an internationally known filmmaker. His hour-long documentary *Hip-Hop: Beyond Beats and Rhymes*, made in conjunction with the Independent Television Service, examines how manhood, sexism, and homophobia (hatred of homosexuals) are presented in hip-hop culture. It looks at hip-hop through the eyes of a fan, specifically focusing on the tendency of some hip-hop to suggest that manhood or masculinity requires "real men" to bash girls, women, and gays. The film was a 2006 Sundance Film Festival Selection. It was produced for the PBS series *Independent Lens* and aired on February 20, 2007, to kick off the Hip-Hop National Community Engagement campaign. The campaign was designed to educate both kids who buy and listen to rap and who watch music videos, and those who make them, about the potential harm of some of the messages being presented. The film and an extensive program developed around the message of the film are being used as teaching tools in many high schools and in various youth organizations throughout the country. Hurt says: "I made the film to let boys and men know that sexism is unacceptable and that men can and should condemn it."

CONCLUSION

Violence against girls and women is a national and worldwide problem of epic proportions. Acts of domestic violence, dating violence, and especially violence toward women in the military are underreported. The problem of violence against girls and women is actually much worse than it appears. The causes of the violence are many and are deeply rooted in cultures and traditions that imply that women are inferior to men and should therefore be controlled by them. Although laws are in place to punish men who act violently against women, laws are not the solution to the problem. The only way to stop the violence is to teach children at an early age that it is wrong. Older teens, parents, teachers, coaches, religious leaders, and members of the media need to remember that they are setting the example that children and adolescents will follow. This is a grave responsibility for those who want to stop the violence.

aggressor A person who attacks or acts hostilely toward another person.

amnesia Loss of memory.

anthropology The scientific study of the origin and the physical, social, and cultural development and behavior of humans.

chastisement Punishment, especially a beating.

condone To overlook or excuse.

designate To set aside for or assign to.

discriminate To make a difference in the treatment of someone or a group worse than others or better than others, usually because of a prejudice about race, gender, age, ethnicity, or religion.

dysfunctional Unable to function emotionally or properly as a social unit.

entice To tempt, attract, or seduce.

explicit Clear and obvious; having no disguised meaning.

feminist A person, either a man or a woman, who supports legal, economic, and social equality between the sexes.

incidence The extent or frequency of the occurrence of something.

initiative A new measure or program.

mandatory Required or obligatory.

misogyny The hatred of women by men.

morale Mood or spirit.

patriarchy A culture or society characterized by the supremacy of the father in the family.

perpetrator The person responsible for an action.

pornography Obscene, lewd, or immodest photographs, writing, or painting, usually of a sexual nature.

post-traumatic stress disorder (PTSD) An anxiety disorder associated with serious traumatic events and characterized by symptoms of survivor guilt, nightmares, flashbacks, and depression.

prelude An introductory action or event.

restrain To tie up or keep under control in some manner.

spontaneous Acting impulsively without planning.

subordinate One who is lower than someone in rank or status.

systematic Methodical in conduct or performance; well thought out, not spontaneous.

tactics Methods or devices for accomplishing a goal.

Break the Cycle

5200 Century Boulevard, Suite 300

Los Angeles, CA 90045

(310) 286-3366

Web site: http://www.breakthecycle.org

This is a national nonprofit organization that engages, educates, and empowers youth to build lives and communities free from dating and domestic violence.

Canadian Women's Foundation

133 Richmond Street NW, Suite 504

Toronto, ON M5H 2L3

Canada

(416) 365-1444

(866) 293-4483

Web site: http://www.cdnwomen.org

This is Canada's only national public foundation dedicated to improving the lives of women and girls.

Family Violence Prevention Fund

383 Rhode Island Street, Suite 304

San Francisco, CA 94103-5113

(415) 252-8900

Web site: http://www.endabuse.org

The mission of this organization is to prevent violence within the home and in the community and to help those whose lives are devastated by violence.

Men Can Stop Rape

P.O. Box 57144

Washington, DC 20037

(202) 265-6530

Web site: http://www.mencanstoprape.org

The mission of this group is to build young men's capacity to challenge harmful aspects of traditional masculinity in order to prevent men's violence against women.

National Aboriginal Circle Against Family Violence

396 Cooper Street, Suite 301

Ottawa, ON K2P 2H7

Canada

(613) 236-1844

Web site: http://www.nacafv.ca/en/html

The mission of this group is to reduce and someday eliminate family violence in Canada's Aboriginal communities.

National Coalition Against Domestic Violence

1120 Lincoln Street, Suite 1603

Denver, CO 80203

(303) 839-1852

Web site: http://www.ncadv.org

This organization is dedicated to the empowerment of battered women and is committed to the elimination of personal and societal violence in the lives of battered women and their children.

National Domestic Violence Hotline

P.O. Box 161810

Austin, TX 78716

(800) 799-7233

This hotline was established in 1996 as a component of the VAWA and provides crisis intervention, information, and referrals to more than 5,000 shelters and domestic violence programs nationwide.

National Organization for Women

1100 H Street NW, 3rd Floor

Washington, DC 20005

(202) 628-8669

Web site: http://www.now.org

This is the largest organization of feminist activists in the United States. Its goal is to take action to bring about equality of women and to eliminate discrimination, harassment, and violence against women.

National Teen Dating Abuse Helpline

P.O. Box 161810

Austin, TX 78716

(866) 331-9474

This helpline is operated by the National Domestic Violence Hotline and offers real-time, one-on-one support from trained peer advocates.

Rape Abuse and Incest National Network (RAINN)

2000 L Street NW, Suite 406

Washington, DC 20003

(202) 544-1034

Web site: http://www.rainn.org

This network provides information on resources throughout the country for survivors of rape, abuse, and incest. It maintains the National Sexual Assault Hotline, (800) 656-4673.

SAFER (Students Active for Ending Rape)

338 Fourth Street, Ground Floor

Brooklyn, NY 11215

(347) 689-3914

Web site: http://www.safercampus.org

This group provides organizational training and support to college and university students so that they can win improvements to their schools' sexual assault prevention and response activities.

U.S. Department of Justice Office on Violence Against Women

800 K Street NW, Suite 920

Washington, DC 20530

(202) 307-6026

Web site: http://www.usdoj.gov/ovw

The Office on Violence Against Women is responsible for the overall coordination and focus of the U.S. Department of Justice's efforts to combat violence committed against women.

Victims of Violence
211 Pretoria Avenue
Ottawa, ON K1S 1X1
Canada
(888) 606-0000
Web site: http://www.victimsofviolence.on.ca
This Canadian nonprofit, nongovernment-funded charitable organization is dedicated
  to preventing crimes against children.

WEB SITES

Due to the changing nature of Internet links, Rosen
Publishing has developed an online list of Web sites
related to the subject of this book. This site is updated
regularly. Please use this link to access the list:

http://www.rosenlinks.com/wom/viol

Burns, Kate, ed. *Violence Against Women*. Farmington Hills, MI: Greenhaven Press, 2008.

Dressen, Sarah. *Dreamland*. New York, NY: Penguin Group, USA, 2000.

Finn, Alex. *Breathing Under Water*. New York, NY: HarperCollins, 2001.

Levy, Barrie. *In Love and In Danger: A Teen's Guide to Breaking Free of Abusive Relationships*. 3rd ed. New York, NY: Seal Press, 2006.

Miles, Al. *Ending Violence in Teen Dating Relationships*. Minneapolis, MN: Augsburg Fortress Publishers, 2005.

Orr, Tamra. *Frequently Asked Questions About Date Rape (FAQ: Teen Life)*. New York, NY: Rosen Publishing Group, 2007.

Picoult, Jodi. *The Tenth Circle*. New York, NY: Atria Books, 2006.

Piercy, Marge. "Rape Poem." *Circles on the Water*. New York, NY: Knopf, 1990.

Sherman, Michelle, and De Anne Sherman. *Finding My Way: A Teen's Guide to Living with a Parent Who Has Experienced Trauma*. Edina, MN: Beaver's Pond Press, 2006.

Slaughter, Lynn. *Teen Issues—Teen Rapes*. Farmington Hills, MI: Lucent Books, 2004.

Avon Foundation. "Avon Foundation News." June 8,
    2008. Retrieved December 23, 2008 (http://
    www.avoncompany.com/women/news/
    press20080608.html).
Benedict, Helen. "Why Soldiers Rape." 2008. Retrieved
    November 25, 2008 (http://www.inthesetimes.com/
    article/3848).
Burns, Kate, ed. *Violence Against Women*. Farmington
    Hills, MI: Greenhaven Press, 2008.
Burns, Rebecca. "Quotes About Domestic Violence."
    August 15, 2007. Retrieved January 17, 2009
    (http://thelaststraw.wordpress.com/2007/08/15/
    quotes-about-domestic-violence).
Carver, Joseph. "Why Would a Woman Falsely Accuse
    Someone of Rape?" December 3, 2008. Retrieved
    December 28, 2008 (http://counsellingresource.
    com/ask-the-psychologist/2008/12/03/
    false-accusation-of-rape).
Centers for Disease Control and Prevention. "About
    Choose Respect." 2006. Retrieved December 23,
    2008 (http://www.chooserespect.org/scripts/about/
    aboutcr.asp).
Centers for Disease Control and Prevention. "CDC Reports
    the Health-Related Costs of Intimate Partner Violence
    Against Women Exceeds $5.8 Billion Each Year in
    the United States." 2003. Retrieved January 4, 2009

(http://www.cdc.gov/od/oc/media/pressrel/
r030428.htm).

Centers for Disease Control and Prevention.
"Understanding Sexual Violence: Fact Sheet 2007."
Retrieved December 26, 2009 (http://www.cdc.gov/
ncipc/pub-res/images/SV%20Factsheet.pdf).

Clifford, Stephanie. "Teaching Teenagers About
Harassment." *New York Times*, January 26, 2009.
Retrieved January 29, 2009 (http://www.nytimes.
com/2009/01/27/business/media/27adco.html).

Community Crisis Center. "Teen Pregnancy and Sexual
Assault." 2004. Retrieved December 26, 2008
(http://www.crisiscenter.org/TeenPregnancy.html).

Davis, Richard. "Mandatory Arrest: A Flawed Policy
Based on a False Premise." March 31, 2008.
Retrieved January 17, 2009 (http://www.policeone.
com/writers/columnists/RichardDavis/articles/
1679122-Mandatory-arrest-A-flawed-policy-based-on-a-
false-premise).

Deen, Thalif. "Rights: U.N. Takes Lead on Ending Gender
Violence." United Nations, February 26, 2008.
Retrieved November 21, 2008 (http://ipsnews.net/
news.asp?idnews=41356).

Dreazen, Yochi. "Rate of Sexual Assault in Army Prompts
an Effort at Prevention." *Wall Street Journal*, October 3,
2008. Retrieved December 13, 2008 (http://online.
wsj.com/article/SB122298757937200069.html).

Family Violence Prevention Fund. "Coaching Boys Into Men Media Campaign." 2000. Retrieved December 16, 2008 (http://www.endabuse.org/section/programs/public_communications/_coaching_boys).

Family Violence Prevention Fund. "Domestic Violence Is a Serious, Widespread Social Problem in America: The Facts." 2008. Retrieved December 2, 2008 (http://endabuse.org/content/action_center/detail/754).

Family Violence Prevention Fund. "History of the Violence Against Women Act." 2000. Retrieved December 4, 2008 (http://endabuse.org/vawa/display.php?DocID=34005).

Family Violence Prevention Fund. "Teen Dating Violence Grant Recipients Announced." November 26, 2008. Retrieved December 16, 2008 (http://www.endabuse.org/content/news/detail/1016).

Feminist Majority Foundation. "Domestic Violence Facts." 2007. Retrieved December 9, 2008 (http://feminist.org/other/dv/dvfact.html).

Goldman, Russell. "Female Veterans Seek Treatment for Sexual Assault." ABC News, October 31, 2007. Retrieved December 12, 2008 (http://abcnews.go.com/US/story?id=3797346&page=1).

Hardcastle, Mike. "What Every Guy Must Know About Date Rape." Retrieved November 25, 2008 (http://teenadvice.about.com/od/daterape/a/daterapeguysfyi.htm).

Independent Television Service. "Hip-Hop: Beyond Beats and Rhyme." 2008. Retrieved December 18, 2008 (http://www.itvs.org/outreach/hiphop/gender.html).

Jenny, C., T. Hooton, A. Bowers, M. Copass, J. Drieger, S. Hillier, N. Kiviatt, L. Corey, W. Stamm, and K. Holmes. "Sexually Transmitted Diseases in Victims of Rape." *New England Journal of Medicine*, Vol. 322, No. 11, March 15, 1990, pp. 462–470.

Katz, Jackson. *The Macho Paradox*. Napersville, IL: Sourcebooks, 2006.

Kaufman, Miriam. "Care of the Adolescent Sexual Assault Victim." *Pediatrics*, Vol. 122, August 2008, pp. 462–470.

Landau, Elaine. *Date Violence*. New York, NY: Franklin Watts, 2004.

Linquist, Scott. *The Date Rape Prevention Book*. Naperville, IL: Sourcebooks, 2000.

Liz Claiborne, Inc. "Love Is Not Abuse." 2008. Retrieved December 16, 2008 (http://www.loveisnotabuse.com/index.html).

London Abused Women's Center. "Theories of Abuse." Retrieved December 19, 2008 (http://lawc.on.ca/ResourceTheoriesBattering.htm).

Mayo Clinic. "Domestic Violence Toward Women: Recognize the Patterns and Seek Help." 2007. Retrieved December 9, 2008 (http://www.mayoclinic.com/health/domestic-violence/WO00044).

McElroy, Wendy. "False Rape Accusations May Be More Common Than Thought." FOX News, May 2, 2006. Retrieved December 28, 2008 (http://www.foxnews.com/story/0,2933,194032,00.html).

Milne, Celia. "Breakup Blast: Rejection Can Trigger a Brain 'Primed to Do Something Dangerous.'" July 25, 2006. Retrieved December 20, 2008 (http://www.macleans.ca/science/technology/article.jsp?content=20060731_131152_131152).

Navarro, Mireya. "State Hopes Statutory Rape Crackdown Will Fight Teen Pregnancy." May 19, 1996. Retrieved December 26, 2008 (http://www.happinessonline.org/BeFaithfulToYourSexualPartner/p14.htm).

Newman, Amie. "Congress Hears Voices of Sexual Assault Survivors in Military." July 31, 2008. Retrieved December 13, 2008 (http://www.rhrealitycheck.org/blog/2008/07/31/congress-hears-voices-sexual-assault-survivors-military).

Office of Violence Against Women. "Fact Sheets." U.S. Department of Justice, 2007. Retrieved November 21, 2008 (http://www.ovw.usdoj.gov/ovw-fs.htm).

O'Leary, Daniel. "Psychological Abuse: A Variable Deserving Critical Attention in Domestic Violence." *Violence and Victims*, Vol. 14, No. 1, Spring 1999, pp. 3–23.

Olson, Elizabeth. "Killings Prompt Efforts to Spot and Reduce Abuse of Teenagers in Dating." *New York Times*, January 4, 2009, p. 12, col. 1.

Ophelia Project. "Relational Aggression." Retrieved February 8, 2009 (http://www.opheliaproject.org/main/relational_aggression.htm).

Price, Diana. "Women's Rights Violations Still Pervasive in U.S. Military." National Organization for Women, August 29, 2006. Retrieved November 25, 2008 (http://www.now.org/issues/military/082906 sexualassault.html).

Rape, Abuse, and Incest National Network. "Congress Passes Important Anti-Rape Legislation." September 27, 2008. Retrieved December 3, 2008 (http://www.rainn.org/news-room/sexual-assault-news/Debby-Smith-Act-reauthorized).

Rape, Abuse, and Incest National Network. "Statistics: Frequency of Sexual Assault." 2006. Retrieved December 14, 2008 (http://www.rainn.org/get-information).

Rape, Abuse, and Incest National Network. "Who Are the Victims?" 2008. Retrieved December 3, 2008 (http://www.rainn.org/get-information/statistics/sexual-assault-victims).

Ritchey, Julia. "Reports of Sexual Assault in U.S. Military Increased in 2008." Voice of America, March 8, 2009. Retrieved March 19, 2009 (http://www.voanews.com/english/2009-03-18-voa70.cfm?rss=politics).

Rosen, Ruth. "The Hidden War on Women in Iraq." Women's International League for Peace and Freedom, July 13, 2006. Retrieved December 29, 2008 (http://www.peacewomen.org/news/Iraq/July06/ The_hidden_war_on_women.html).

Russell, Diana. *The Politics of Rape*. Lincoln, NE: iUniverse, 2003.

Saar, Malika Saada. "A Missing Piece of the Prevention Puzzle." Center for American Progress, August 6, 2008. Retrieved December 2, 2009 (http://www. americanprogress.org/issues/2008/08/missing_ piece.html).

Sampson, Ovelta. "Girls Talk! 'Relational Aggression' as Harmful as Any Schoolyard." *Gazette* (Colorado Springs), April 29, 2002. Retrieved February 8, 2009 (http://findarticles.com/p/articles/mi_qn4191/ is_20020429/ai_n100c).

Spilbor, Jonna. "Is the Recent Spate of High-Profile Teen Pregnancies, Including Bristol Palen's, Jamie Lynn Spears's, Telling Us It's Time to Alter Statutory Rape Laws?" Find Law, September 16, 2008. Retrieved December 26, 2008 (http://writ.lp.findlaw.com/ commentary/20080916_spilbor.html).

Stephenson, Karen. "False Allegations." May 14, 2007. Retrieved December 28, 2008 (http://abuse. suite101.com/article.cfm/false_allegations).

Students Against Violence Everywhere. "History." 2007. Retrieved December 16, 2008 (http://www. nationalsave.org/main/history.php).

Teen Advice. "Date Rape Drugs: Date Rape Drugs Explained and De-mystified." Retrieved November 25, 2008 (http://teenadvice.about.com/library/weekly/ aa062502a.htm).

Texas Association Against Sexual Assault. "Students Taking Action for Respect." 2008. Retrieved December 28, 2008 (http://www.taasa.org/star).

Tjaden, Patricia, and Nancy Thoennes. "Extent, Nature, and Consequences of Intimate Partner Violence." National Institute of Justice, July 2000. Retrieved January 18, 2009 (http://www.ojp.usdoj/nij/ pubs-sum/181867.htm).

Ulene, Valerie. "For Many Rape Victims, Treatment and Support Services Fall Short." *Los Angeles Times*, October 6, 2008. Retrieved December 26, 2008 (http://articles.latimes.com/2008/oct/06/health/ he-themd6).

United Nations. "Declaration on the Elimination of Violence Against Women." 1993. Retrieved December 16, 2008 (http://www.stopvaw.org/Declaration_on_the_ Elimination_of_Violence_Against_Women3).

U.S. Census Bureau. "Midyear Population by Age and Sex for 2010." Retrieved December 18, 2008 (http:// www.census.gov/cgi-bin/ipc/agggen).

Willens, Jake. "Women in the Military: Combat Roles
    Considered." 1996. Retrieved December 29, 2008
    (http://www.cdi.org/issues/women/combat.html).
WomensHealth.gov. "Violence Against Women: Domestic
    and Intimate Partner Violence." 2007. Retrieved
    December 3, 2009 (http://www.womenshealth.gov/
    violence/types/domestic.cfm).
Wright, Ann. "Military Town Newspaper Challenges U.S.
    Military in Murder of Military Women." October 17,
    2008. Retrieved November 25, 2008 (http://www.
    truthout.org/101708J).

INDEX

violence against women by
members of, 9, 65–68,
70–73
violence against women within,
68–70, 71, 73, 74–75, 89
military culture, and rape,
70–71, 72
Military Domestic and Sexual
Violence Response Act,
75–77
military sexual trauma, 74–75
misogyny, 71, 78
Mosley, Ortralla, 83

N

National Domestic Violence
Hotline, 28, 80
Native Americans, and rape, 37

O

Office on Violence Against
Women, 10, 13, 80
Ophelia Project, 11
Orange, Alex, 86

P

physical abuse
as aspect of domestic violence,
13–14, 19, 52
and dating, 50, 52
physical sexual violence, 30, 33
poverty, and sexual assault, 36–37

psychological abuse
as aspect of domestic violence,
13, 16–17
and dating, 50
stalking as, 30

R

rape, 8, 14, 33, 49
consequences of, 40–44
date rape, 49, 52–59
false accusations of, 45–48
and the military, 67–68,
70–72, 74–77
and pregnancy, 41, 44–45
reasons behind, 53, 72
statistics on, 33, 36–38, 41,
42, 44, 45, 53, 54
statutory, 41
and teens, 40, 41, 52, 53,
54–55
and victims put on trial, 79–80
vulnerability factors for, 33–38
ways to prevent, 53
what to do if you are raped,
59–63
Rape, Abuse, and Incest National
Network (RAINN), 44, 53
rape trauma syndrome, 41–42
Rebecca Project for Human
Rights, 45
relational aggression, 11
religion, and violence against
women, 7
Robert Woods Johnson
Foundation, 85

ABOUT THE AUTHOR

Linda Bickerstaff is a retired general and peripheral vascular surgeon who has cared for victims of domestic violence, dating violence, and sexual assault in emergency rooms and operating rooms. She also has a dear friend whose life was threatened by an abusive husband. It has taken years for the friend to escape the nightmares of that experience. Bickerstaff has written several books for Rosen Publishing, including *Cocaine: Coke and the War on Drugs* (Drug Abuse and Society) and *Modern-Day Slavery* (In the News).

PHOTO CREDITS